THE GIFTS OF
THE FAIRY MELUSINE

by

Barak A. Bassman

TELEMACHUS PRESS

This book is a work of fiction. Names, characters, places and incidents are either the product of the author's imagination or are used fictitiously. Any resemblance to actual persons, living or dead, or to actual events or locales is entirely coincidental.

THE GIFTS OF THE FAIRY MELUSINE

Cover designed by Telemachus Press, LLC

Cover image licensed pursuant to https://commons.wikimedia.org/wiki/File:Fougères_(35)_Église_SaintSulpice_Baie_06_Fi chier_02.jpg. Information on the creator of the image is available through this link. Please note the creator and licensor of the image has in no way reviewed or approved of the book or any of its contents.

Published by Telemachus Press, LLC
7652 Sawmill Road
Suite 304
Dublin, Ohio 43016
http: //www.telemachuspress.com

ISBN: 978-1-948046-36-7 (eBook)
ISBN: 978-1-948046-37-4 (paperback)
ISBN: 978-1-948046-38-1 (hardback)

Library of Congress Control Number: 2018964311

FICTION / Folklore

Version 2018.11.15

Table of Contents

The Gifts of the Fairy Melusine

I. How the Fairy Melusine
Put Raymond Back Together Again

REUVEN WAS SURPRISED when he opened his eyes and found his limbs stitched back together again. The last thing he recalled was being on the steps of the cathedral in the town of … well … the town whose name he could not remember, but there had been a grey cathedral and he had been on its steps when the armed men, with visors pulled low, reached for their swords and severed his head, arms, and legs from his torso. Although everything had happened so suddenly that he did not have time to try to escape, he still had the presence of mind, in his severed head, to register the fact of his own death before the world went dark.

Yet now, unmistakably, he could feel his body put back together again, and warm, flower-scented air filled his lungs. With a slight effort he sat up and looked around. His clothes had changed—he was now wearing a soft white robe—and he was sitting on wet grass, near a stream, in a forest. A deer darted by in the distance. Grabbing a low-hanging tree branch, Reuven pulled himself upright.

A woman's voice, light as a pebble skipping on the surface of the water, reached his ears: Not too much all at once, it is a great strain on a human body to be taken apart and re-assembled. Breathe slowly and walk with small steps.

He turned toward the direction of the voice. There he saw a tall woman—taller than him—with yellow, almost white, hair that fell far below her shoulders. She, too, wore a white robe, almost identical to his.

Where am I? Reuven asked. Is this the World to Come?

No, the lady replied, this is the same Earth you have lived upon all your life. I found the pieces of you scattered on the cathedral steps. But towns are no places for wounds to heal and for things that have been severed to be reattached, so I brought you here and put you back together.

Who are you? Are you some kind of demon?

The lady looked down and visibly composed herself. My name is Melusine, and I can bestow certain wondrous gifts upon the man who will agree to love me. And what is your name, sir? Are you pledged to love another woman already?

I am Reuven, he replied. And my wife, may her memory be a blessing, is surely dead.

Melusine's body relaxed. She playfully frowned and tilted her head to the side before responding: Reuven is not a fitting name for my lover—it has the wrong timbre and will not go over well. No, you were baptized at that cathedral, so Reuven you can no longer be—I know this, I smelled the sweet waters of baptism mixed in with the blood curdled about your head. You can be my Raymond.

Now, Raymond, will you agree to love me?

The man closed his eyes. In his mind he saw his wife, his Jael, cradling their little son in her arms?

it was a few weeks ago, at night—Gershom had wheezed from a bad cough in his chest and could not sleep, so Jael had rocked him in the moonlight. He suppressed the urge to sob, reminding himself that Jael and Gershom were in Paradise now.

He opened his eyes again. Where was he? Was this place real? With his family murdered, the world felt distant and dreamlike—as though he were perched in the high tree branches watching himself amble about in the forest below. Maybe he was in Paradise dreaming? But why would he dream of this isolated place, all alone except for this woman whom he had never met and who was not Jael?

Melusine pressed her case further:

You must think I'm beautiful, no? Everyone always said I was beautiful. And I can give you gifts, so many gifts: wealth, land, castles, nobility, sons. You will be a mighty lord with a resplendent court, and I will be your beautiful queen. Just agree to love me.

Why me? the man asked. Why not choose some bold knight with a handsome face and an intact body? Or the fine-looking son of a lord? Why not let a poor Jewish soul rest and be with his kin in the World to Come?

Melusine sighed and smiled sadly. She looked at her fingernails for a moment and then answered him:

It is of the greatest importance that I be loved by a mortal man with an immortal soul. I could never trust a man whom I had not forged with my own hands—a man made by other hands would fly away from a creature like me, if not now then later on. You don't need to feel pain anymore. I will show you the bliss of a life without the hardships you have endured.

The man leaned against a tree and carefully studied Melusine. She looked and sounded real, and she was far more beautiful than any woman he had ever seen before. He had loved his Jael, she was a pious, upright woman, but she was a woman with sweat dripping on top of her chapped lips and acne here and there. Melusine reminded him of a picture of the Garden of Eden in a manuscript he had once seen in a monastery where he had been delivering barrels of wine. The artist's rendering of Eve had been so lithe and pale and blond, without a blemish, just like the lady before him now.

At that moment his limbs ached and his belly knotted with hunger pain. His reborn body yearned for soft things—beds, blankets, warm delicacies to eat, sweet airy wines to drink, maybe even a woman's arms to cradle and rock him like a small boy again. Perhaps, the man wondered, there was a greater purpose here—how could the miracle of his resurrection have occurred without the intervention of the higher realms?

He looked closely at Melusine. Her expression was filled with hope and anxiety. She seemed, for whatever mad reason, actually to need him to pledge his love to her. As he mulled matters over in silence, her eyes had begun to quiver and she had turned her gaze bashfully toward the ground. He thought: How can I be so cruel as to deny her what she needs so much?

Jael and Gershom had died as martyrs for the sanctification of the Holy Name, cut down with so many other pillars of their righteous generation of Israel by the ruthless Crusader knights on their way to plunder and ravage Jerusalem. There was no home to which he could return, just dirty ashes and guilty Christian neighbors who would not want to be reminded of the slaughters they had so recently cheered on against all those Jewish women and children.

So why not agree to love this woman? Could she be worse than the murderers he had left behind?

The man walked gingerly towards Melusine and spoke to her in a choked whisper: I will love you, and I will be Raymond for you.

Melusine smiled broadly and took both of his hands into hers. She led him through the forest, over streams and rocks, around trees, between docile sleepy wolves, until they arrived at an open meadow blindingly lit up by the sun high in the sky. Raymond was certain he had been floating on air, and that Melusine was a winged fairy queen.

She sat him down on a wide log and, standing next to him, faced the meadow. Her hands fluttered rapidly in bizarre gestures and she uttered guttural, animalistic sounds from her almost closed mouth. Stones began falling from the sky—not rough jagged boulders but carefully hewn, perfectly square blocks, which descended slowly toward the ground to pile neatly on top of each other. After an hour or so, he could make out the rough outline of a stronghold. Soon enough, a full-fledged castle stood constructed in front of him.

Melusine stopped speaking in her strange animal language and let her hands rest at her sides. A look of satisfaction bubbled up on her face as she briefly surveyed the new castle. Her hands now cupped together and rose to meet her lips. A harsh, nasal sound blasted forth from her throat, like a thousand crows screaming. This sound was answered by several trumpets blown from the ramparts of the castle.

The castle gates swung open and a gracefully dressed, haughty old man rode out on a white horse flanked by four knights in glinting white armor. Raymond was sure this was his true death coming for him now—this witch with her other-worldly beauty was no doubt a demon who had been sent to test him, and he had failed, and now he was to be brutally dispatched to *gehenna*, to Hell.

The elderly gentleman and his knights rode up to Raymond. The man dismounted and knelt down before him, kissing his wrist in obeisance and addressing him in florid tones:

My lord, Count Raymond, your humble servants joyously greet you upon your safe return to your lands and to your castle. We have made up your bed and prepared a feast for you and the Lady Melusine. Do not look so alarmed, my lord, we are here to serve you. It will be a festive celebration tonight. Tomorrow the many noble guests will arrive for your wedding.

Although baffled by this speech, Raymond obediently followed this man who claimed to be his servant through the castle gates, with Melusine walking by his side. Inside the castle courtyard he saw great multitudes of men, women, and children bustling about with food, wine barrels, firewood, tapers, furniture, and weapons. Everywhere he turned he was greeted as the honored and revered lord of the castle. The elegant old man led him up the stairs of the castle's keep to a bed chamber. Raymond threw himself down on the soft white sheets—which were far more luxurious than any bedding he had ever touched before—and collapsed into a deep sleep.

The old servant roused him several hours later to wash and dress for supper. After readying himself with no little assistance from this same servant (who was far more knowledgeable of the ins and outs of the attire of noblemen), Raymond was led into a great hall with a long, narrow table, where he was seated next to Melusine.

He finally worked up the courage to speak: What is this place? Where are we? And who are all these men and women rushing to and fro?

Melusine calmly replied that they were at home and that he was the lord of this castle.

How is that possible? I have never been lord of anything but the wine barrels in which I trade as a merchant.

You are a lord because I was born a noble lady, and I insist that my husband be a lord. I am pleased with how our castle has come together.

A steaming plate of food was placed in front of him, which, the servant informed him, was a choice leg of boar hunted that very day.

Raymond blanched at the meat and could not touch it.

What is wrong, my love? Melusine asked. It is delicious. Our cook is quite talented, and the meat is fresh.

But I cannot eat this meat. It is unclean, forbidden. I need kosher meat.

My love, you are a Christian lord. This is what Christian lords eat. You were baptized and you pledged your love to me. You are freed of the old laws, forget them and delight in my gifts.

Raymond looked at her pale grey eyes, so beseeching and alluring. Melusine ran her hand through her golden hair. The smell of the seasoned meat drifted to his nose and it too tempted him.

He recalled how, before she had resurrected him, he had been baptized. A group of Crusader knights had grabbed him by the neck and dragged him into the church. They had held his head above the baptismal font and demanded of him— would he accept baptism or death?

There were Jewish corpses lying on the ground nearby, freshly killed, who had clearly refused baptism. Looking into those lifeless eyes staring blankly at nothingness, his courage had failed him and, to his great shame, he had submitted to baptism. He felt his cowardice had been justly rewarded when, upon later exiting that same church, he was nonetheless marked as a Jew by other marauding knights who quickly hacked him to pieces on the cathedral steps.

Yet now he was lord of this castle and expected to be, if not a good Christian, then certainly not a Jew anymore. He had failed to uphold the honor of the Torah, and he had apostatized, so now his body would be polluted with unclean meat. Perhaps this too was a fit punishment—his insides no longer merited the blessings of kosher food. With a heavy heart, he ate the meat. But he could not look upon Melusine again that night.

The wedding was celebrated the next day. Guests arrived from far and wide, finely dressed lords and ladies whom Melusine greeted effusively, but who were complete strangers to Raymond. He spent the day bewildered, as if he were sleepwalking through someone else's dream. The Christian wedding ceremony was difficult for him to follow, leading the bishop repeatedly (and impatiently) to prompt the dazed groom with the appropriate responses. Then there was a banquet lasting long into the evening, with music, song, and heaping platters of delicacies to eat and barrels of expensive wines to drink.

Yet Raymond took no part in the merriment. He recalled his first wedding, when he was still Reuven. He and Jael had stood under a *chuppah* made of faded and fraying fabric. As she circled him seven times, his heart had palpitated with excitement and growing love. With her nervous and deliberate steps, she had seemed so good and modest and pious. This was his *bashert*, his destined bride, he had been sure of it. Until the Crusaders had come to the Rhineland and sundered her soul from her flesh.

His wedding ring—his true ring, the one Jael had placed on his finger—where was it? He looked at his hand and saw only the jewel-encrusted monstrosity placed upon his hand that day by his new wife. But where was the plain gold band that Jael had put on his finger? Had the Crusaders stripped it from his dead body? Had Melusine?

His yearning for that simple ring overwhelmed Raymond. To avoid making a public spectacle of his grief, he excused himself and returned to his bed chamber to sob into his sheets. Without thinking, he recited the Hebrew *kaddish* prayer for the souls of his dead wife and son. Exhausted from his anguish, he eventually fell asleep.

Melusine woke him sometime after midnight. Although the festivities had ended late, she did not appear joyful.

Raymond, you pledged to love me. I have given you wondrous gifts in exchange for that love. Are you spurning them now? Our noble guests were quite surprised at your behavior, and I had to make many excuses.

I am lost, he replied, with his head still buried in the sheets.

Do you pledge your love to me?

Raymond looked up at her. She was so beautiful, pale and golden-haired in the moonlight, and her eyes were so hopeful. Although he could not fathom why, she needed him, and that raw need coursed through her trembling, pleading features. His soul was suddenly filled with pity and desire for this enchanting creature. He had failed the holy community of Israel by cravenly submitting to baptism and he had been away when his wife and son were murdered by the wicked Crusaders. Yet he had a new chance to live and perhaps he could save Melusine from—from he knew not what, but from whatever the something was that haunted her and filled her with terror and sorrow. He reached out to stroke the silky yellow locks that had fallen carelessly upon his belly.

So Raymond pledged his love once more, with genuine longing and desire in his eyes, and begged her pardon for his behavior—everything had happened so fast, he had been overwhelmed.

No worries, my love. It will be easier as time goes by. As long as you abide by your promise to love me, you will enjoy my gifts. And the one proof of your love that I require is that you swear to me the following: that no matter what, on every Saturday, you will not see me but let me be perfectly alone, wherever I choose, for the entire day.

Raymond replied that he did not understand—why must she be alone then?

It is not for you to understand. Give me your word and prove your love.

And so he did. Melusine, a serene smile on her lips, nestled into the side of her new husband's body, entwined her legs with his, and fell asleep. Raymond stared out the window at the big circular moon and sighed.

II. The Valiant and Chivalrous Sons of the Noble Count Raymond

LIFE—HIS NEW life reborn as a Christian noble—was grand for Count Raymond. In the beginning, he had felt uneasy receiving supplications from, and dispensing justice among, his serfs and vassals, but with time it felt natural to him that he should be greeted with humility and reverence, and that the men and women in his lands should look to him for guidance.

Lady Melusine made sure his every desire was satisfied. When he wished for clothes, she summoned the finest tailors with a snap of her fingers. When he felt hungry, he had merely to pronounce his craving and a page would appear, out of nowhere, bearing exactly the wine he had dreamed of, or the perfectly seasoned and cooked cut of meat he had wanted.

Memories faded of his former life as a Jew. He stopped caring whether food was forbidden by the Torah. While never entirely at ease receiving the Holy Communion or hearing Mass, he carried out these ceremonies as important duties of the local Christian lord. Melusine also helped him in becoming a Christian: She confessed that she too had been raised to pray to different gods, older than the Christian Savior, but she recognized that, in order to avoid unpleasant gossip, she must pay obeisance to the regnant deity and His Church. Her words and example fortified Raymond.

Nevertheless, scurrilous whispers still went around. Count Raymond learned that some unsavory men claimed the new lord flinched when the sacred host touched his tongue, or that he could not look directly into the eyes of the statue of the Holy Virgin in the castle chapel, or that he never wore the sign of the cross anywhere upon his body.

While Raymond tried to ignore these rumors and even convinced himself he had done a fine job of pretending to be a Christian, it seemed to him that Melusine was all too aware of what was said about her husband and the danger if his true origins were revealed. She diverted attention away from her husband's uneasy embrace of his new faith by founding numerous convents, monasteries, and hermitages, and by purchasing, at tremendous expense, holy relics from blessed saints to adorn them and draw pilgrims.

Melusine also offered something more tantalizing to the Church: the ability to influence the future of her domains. She had borne twin boys to Raymond, whom she named Guyon and Renaud. Their education and upbringing were handed over to the direction of the family confessor, who, confident of the Church's influence over the future heirs to Raymond's lands, became a fervent supporter of Raymond and Melusine and denounced any libelous rumors about the supposed laxity in the noble couple's faith.

Raymond at first resisted handing over his sons' up-bringing to the Church. Yet when Melusine pressed that the Church was in the best position to fill them with learning, wisdom, and piety, he failed to find the words to rebut her. He somehow felt it was wrong to have priests instructing his sons, instead of their father. He wanted to say he should be trusted with the raising of his own sons, but then had to admit to himself that he was woefully deficient in the basic knowledge that his sons would need. He had barely any grasp of Christian doctrine and, at best, stumbled clumsily through Mass and confession. He had no idea how to bear arms or ride a horse, and his lack of courtly manners was purposefully concealed beneath an icy, taciturn reserve. And so he felt compelled to yield to the wishes of the Lady Melusine.

Yet his life remained sweet in its many delights. Through the years Melusine never aged one day, and she remained as young and beautiful and passionate as on their wedding night. When Raymond felt weary, her moist, honeyed kiss upon his dried lips would miraculously restore his youthfulness and vitality. He strictly followed his vow to leave her completely alone on Saturdays, even though some Saturdays he yearned achingly for the sight of her lovely, graceful figure.

His days were largely spent managing his estates and dispensing justice. Fortunately, Melusine had chosen to gift him with vineyards, so that his years as a Jewish wine merchant were put to good use. And he found he had a knack for handling legal disputes. Instead of issuing harsh and swift decrees, as did many of his fellow lords in their haste to return to hunting, he listened slowly and carefully to each disagreement and asked probing questions to try to find common ground. In this manner, Raymond was able to mediate more than he judged, and often as not helped the disputants reach a settlement on terms that each respected. As he brokered more and more amicable resolutions and healed bitter divides, he became greatly beloved in the countryside for his wisdom and mercy. He even once saw Melusine blush when she heard the castle servants praise her husband's justice.

In the beginning, Raymond had been unsure what to do in his spare time. He had no desire to hunt, as he could not bear the thought of watching an animal die (and he was terrified that his horse would throw him hard into a tree trunk since he did not know how to ride). He would pace his castle courtyard and gardens, itching for something to occupy his mind.

When he had been the Jew Reuven, he had studied a page or two of the Jewish Bible, the *Tanakh*, each day with whatever commentaries were at hand in the synagogue or *bet midrash* in which he found himself. His eyes hungered to feast lovingly again upon Hebrew letters and his soul yearned to hear the words of Abraham, Moses, David, and Solomon.

But for a Christian lord, Hebrew texts were out of the question—too many suspicious mouths would wonder how he had acquired such unusual knowledge. Still, as a merchant who had sold fine wines to princes and bishops, Raymond had long been proficient in Latin. So he purchased a beautifully copied manuscript of the Church's Bible, the Latin Vulgate as translated by Saint Jerome. The books of the Vulgate were off-putting at first. Not only did Latin letters and phrases replace the true Hebrew originals—imposter letters for an imposter as a Christian lord, he reflected—but the pages were filled with illustrations of the text that struck him as bizarre and grotesque.

For example, Raymond had always believed he had known what King David looked like: a huge lion of a man, broad, muscular, sweaty and dusty, with a heavy sword swaying from his waist and battle-scars on his face, a terrible warrior prince who had not hesitated to slaughter Israel's enemies and to establish a great kingdom by brute force. He was no Saul, too timid to kill the Amalekites to the last soul, no, King David—*David Melech Yisrael*—was the Holy One's ruthless and invincible outstretched arm of vengeance and conquest.

Yet the copyist of this Vulgate manuscript illustrated King David in the likeness of his supposed distant descendant, the crucified Savior: pale, gaunt, with large watery eyes imploring heaven as he played his golden harp. Raymond was baffled—how could anyone who had read the plain words of the holy texts imagine that Israel's mightiest warrior looked like a half-starved, lovesick minstrel?

To his amazement, all of Israel's mighty heroes—Abraham and Jacob, Moses and Joshua, Solomon and David, even Samson and Barak—were depicted in the manuscript as ethereal and waifish. It was their enemies who were muscular, lithe, and sensual, with hard and lustful eyes focused on this world and its pleasures.

He perused the Church's officially sanctioned Bible commentaries, which only mystified him further. According to the Church, nothing in the Bible actually was what it was. Instead, everything was allegory and allusion: Israel was not Israel; Israel was the Church. All the tales of ancient Israel were in fact subtle references to and predictions of the future life of

Jesus, and so on and so forth. This entire way of reading the Bible—where Jews were not Jews—struck him as even more of a fraud than the usurping Latin letters pretending to do the work of the magical Hebrew letters.

So Count Raymond closed the Church's commentaries and covered the ridiculous illustrations with his hand, and concentrated instead on the writings he loved. He soon relaxed his censure of the Latin letters and even grew fond of Saint Jerome's Latin style. In his solitary hours under smoky tapers in the castle library, he reclaimed his sacred, beloved texts and let his imagination roam freely about the hills and valleys of the Holy Land. While his devotion to the Old Testament earned him the praise of the Church and the populace (although his confessor was puzzled at his disinterest in the New Testament), to Raymond, these were the times when he and the Vulgate Bible could lay down their artful deceits and pretenses and breathe the air of clear truth with each other.

And thus he passed many gilded, but lonely, years. While his beautiful wife Melusine gifted him with every worldly luxury and honor, and kissed him with lips sweet as late summer peaches, he was never comfortable speaking with his fellow nobles (who lacked his passion for the Bible and preferred to swap hunting exploits), and given his now high station, he could not relate to the common people. He felt that the people around him, Melusine included, were sealed away from him, inaccessible, and he watched and spoke to them through window panes in a room where he had accidently been trapped. The great men of the Old Testament—Joseph and Elijah and Samuel and Job—all felt so much more real and alive to him.

In his solitary musings Raymond often lost track of his sons Guyon and Renaud. Given that Melusine had insisted on the Church directing their upbringing, he had been careful not to interfere in their activities. But what had started as caution became habit: He saw his boys rarely, sometimes not for days, as they were tutored by priests or, as they grew, by professional soldiers who trained them to ride horses and fight with swords and lances.

It did not help that Guyon and Renaud looked the way that they did. Count Raymond was a short, wiry man with brown hair and brown eyes. His first wife Jael had been even shorter, with wide hips, thick eyebrows, and almost black eyes. Their little Gershom had been like his parents: small, weak, and dark.

Guyon and Renaud, by contrast, were strapping: tall, broad blond boys with light blue eyes who seemed born to ride horses and fell boars in the forest. By age twelve the boys towered over their puny father, who flinched when they rode their fast horses too near to him. The boys commanded instant respect wherever they went, and loved to joust and to hunt—but, despite their clerical upbringing, they could not bear the fusty smell of old manuscripts.

Count Raymond could not understand how he had sired two sons such as these. Nor was he alone in wondering from whence their robust blondeness had come: Many tongues wagged that Melusine went off in secret on Saturdays for trysts with a lover, who was the boys' real father. How else to explain how little they resembled their so-called father? Raymond did his best not to think about such things, although he could never fully put his mind at ease.

Nevertheless, uncomfortable as the boys made him, Raymond would smile and praise them, and try to make idle, inoffensive chatter. These conversations were not easy: The boys, with great excitement, would talk about a new horse, or how they had killed a rabbit, and as they rapidly droned on, Raymond found his mind wandering—which became all too obvious when Guyon or Renaud, out of breath, asked their father a question about something they had recounted, but he had no idea what had been said. The joy then faded from the boys' faces, and he felt ashamed before their disappointment.

He reminded himself that Gershom was dead, martyred, and that these were his sons now, and he had to be a good father to them. Part of him longed to teach them Hebrew prayers and how to build a *sukkah*, as his father had taught him, but, no, he was a Christian father now. What, he wondered, did Christian noblemen fathers teach their sons? The ways of heaven and the intricacies of sacred texts were the prerogatives of the priests—not that his sons cared to study these matters too much anyway.

So what was he supposed to teach his sons? To ride horses, to plunge lances into foes, to hunt game? But he knew none of these things. Count Raymond was certain that, from the vantage point of his sons and their noble born friends, he was an eccentric and inept failure of a lord and father, unable to be the kind of man they expected him to be. His boys wanted to be swaggering warriors riding powerful horses, and all he did was embarrass them with his squinting eyes and hesitant gait.

Sometimes Raymond tried to evade the dutiful side of fatherhood and simply exuded tenderness. When the boys were little, he would chase them around the castle courtyard before scooping them in his arms, squeezing them, and covering their cheeks and foreheads with the wet, sticky kisses of an old Jewish father. Yet as they grew, and learned the ways of lords and knights, Guyon and Renaud became embarrassed at their father's unmanly affections. While they never spoke a harsh word to him, Raymond could see how they braced themselves and frowned when he approached with wide arms outstretched, and those cold, impatient glares cut him to the quick. Hence, as they grew older, Raymond often kept his distance from his disapproving and disappointed sons.

As time wore on and his spirit was weighted down with harsh loneliness, he also drifted away from Melusine. He could not help asking himself so many what-ifs: What if Melusine had not revived him from the dead? Had he been close to reaching the World to Come when she had collected his body parts and grabbed his soul before it had fully ascended? Would he have joined Jael and Gershom in Paradise along with the other martyrs, if only Melusine had left him in peace?

Raymond told himself he should be grateful for his wife. She was far more beautiful than any other woman he had ever beheld, certainly more than Jael with her square, short body and greasy horsehair wig that never did sit quite right on her head. And Melusine was always obliging. Anything she thought he wanted—lands, titles, children, delicacies, fine clothes, passionate embraces—she gave him willingly, joyfully, with a look of such hopefulness on her face, as if she needed his approval the way he needed water and air.

But no matter how long they were married, he felt her to be a stranger. She would not speak of her past, and offered no explanation for her secret retreats each Saturday. When he would try to tell her of his past as a Jew, and how he missed the melodies of the chanting of the Torah, she would put two fingers on his lips and whisper into his ear that he should forget his dishonorable, lowly past and rejoice that he had been raised to such a great station. Let go of your old pain, she cooed, love me and live reborn as a more honored, a more exalted man.

Yet Raymond could not let go of his old world. He tried speaking to Melusine of the wondrous tales of the Old Testament. One night he spoke enraptured about how the righteous prophet Elijah, a pillar of his generation, had vanquished the seductive pagan Queen Jezebel and her many hundreds of priests of Baal. Their false god could not summon fire to their altar, whereas Elijah's prayer to the Holy One, Blessed be He, the one true living God, immediately set His altar aflame. Raymond recounted with glee how Elijah, triumphant, ordered the deaths of the priests of Baal and overcame the lies of Jezebel. But when he looked down again at Melusine, she was fast asleep. At that moment, his heart burst with hatred of his lovely wife.

Nonetheless, the comforts of the life Melusine had given him, the pleasures of all those luxuries and delicacies, sustained him as one day followed the next. Year after year passed, until the time came when Guyon and Renaud, by then eighteen years old, approached their father in the castle courtyard and asked to speak with him.

Of course, he replied.

Guyon spoke for the brothers: Father, we seek your permission to take the cross and ride with our fellow Christian knights to the Holy Land, to fight the wicked nonbelievers there. We wish to share in the glory and the blessings of the Church's great Crusade. We are wasting away right now because there are no noble adventures to pursue here. This land is blessed with peace, so you don't need warriors to ride forth and do battle for your honor. The fight is against the deniers of our Savior who would defile the Holy Land. Please let us go, give your consent. We will return covered in renowned and mighty deeds, we swear to you, and the prestige of our house will be all the greater.

Count Raymond staggered backwards at these words, and caught a branch in his hand to break his fall. He looked away— he could not bear the sight of their big blond bodies and dangling jeweled scabbards. He tried to speak, but his throat constricted and his temples pounded. He fell to his knees, vomited, and lost consciousness.

He awoke in his soft bed, with Melusine stroking his cheek. You have been ill, she said, you have been delirious with a fever for a week. But I finally discerned how to break it, and I have lifted the affliction from your flesh. While you were indisposed, I gave my consent, in your name, for Guyon and Renaud to take the cross and join the holy Crusade. There is no need to worry, my love. I gave them each a magical stone, hung around their necks and touching their breasts, which will make them invulnerable to harm in battle. They will return home, covered in glory, and our noble house will be admired far and wide. You can spend your old age basking in the heroism of such sons.

Raymond looked away from Melusine and stared at a blank white wall. In his mind's eye, he saw a small, dark-haired boy—his son, his other son, the one whom he loved, Gershom—reach for the cup of wine he had just blessed to welcome the holy Shabbat. And his eyes were soon awash with quiet tears.

III. Zakhor

RAYMOND FOUND COMFORT in the stillness at
midnight. The full white moon shone brightly overhead in the
castle courtyard where even the sentries had dozed off. He
thought of the many lonely midnights he had spent in this
castle conjured by Melusine's magic. Her refusal to speak of
any past, his or hers, had slowly walled him off from any true
human connection. He felt less like a man, with sorrows and
joys, than like another prop fabricated from Melusine's strange
powers to adorn—to adorn what? What was the point of all of
this? Why had she chosen him, who was such a poor fit for a
life of noble feats in Christendom?

He closed his eyes and tried to remember a happy midnight. There he was years ago, a runt of a boy named Reuven,
with his father Shimon, by the banks of the Rhine. It was
midnight and his father had woken to pray. Reuven had secretly followed him outside—he was supposed to stay
asleep—until Shimon reached a clearing near the river. Reuven
hid behind a bush and watched as his father swayed and
chanted in Hebrew in his deep guttural voice. The boy felt that

the words from his father's lips floated over to where he was crouched on the ground, covering him like a soft blanket. He had wanted that moment to last forever.

When Shimon turned around, he saw Reuven in the bushes. The boy froze in terror certain he was to reap just retribution for his bad behavior. But Shimon smiled, picked his small son up in his arms and planted a wet, reassuring kiss on Reuven's forehead. Reuven thanked the Holy One, Blessed be He, for helping his father see that he only was curious and not up to any mischief.

There was a fierce argument the next morning when Reuven's mother learned what had happened. She fumed: The boy could have caught his death out there! And what if an animal had bitten him? Or he had twisted his ankle?

Shimon smiled his resigned smile that his son now remembered so well. But those terrors did not come to pass. Because Reuven, good boy that he is, put his faith and trust in the Holy One, Blessed be He, Who saw that he only wished to honor his father down here and the Glorious and Exalted Name above. If it had been decreed in the higher realms that it was Reuven's time, then he would have departed from this world whether he was by the river, in his bed, or sitting on a tree top.

His mother stormed out of the house to complain to the other mothers about how she had been cursed with such a grinning idiot of a husband and how the fool had stupidly endangered their son.

But Shimon got his way, and Reuven now joined him each night for midnight prayers. Reuven loved this ritual. His sisters were not allowed to go out at night, and his friends were not permitted to roam after dark, but he was special. In the beginning he stayed silent, nestling his head in his father's robe and twirling the fringes of his *tallit*. Once he had memorized the prayers, he joined in too—for there was not enough light to read from a prayer book, he had realized, so these prayers could only pass your lips if you concentrated hard on each word and committed it to memory. At the sound of Reuven's squeaky mouse voice, his father would reach down and playfully rub the top of his head.

As the years passed and the boy grew to be a man, these midnights became the time when Reuven and Shimon could speak alone with each other. It was on one such midnight that Shimon told Reuven that his schooling must come to an end. He was old enough now to learn the family wine business. Reuven protested: But I am not ready yet, I still have so much to learn—I have not completed each tractate of the *Gemarah*, my friends will be studying without me.

Shimon assured Reuven that they could study together each day, whatever tractate he desired. The obligation to study does not end when school ends. But a Jew must make a living.

Reuven tried a different tack: I will be of no help to you. I will only get in the way with stupid questions and clumsy actions.

Shimon brushed off this concern too. Of course you will be in the way at first, full of stupidity and clumsiness. But you will learn, and then you will be able to support a wife and children of your own, may you merit such blessings.

And so Reuven, against his will, was propelled into manhood. He traveled with his father through the lands of the Holy Roman Empire and the Kingdom of Hungary inspecting and buying wines, and then reselling the barrels to the princes, lords, and monasteries in the lower Rhineland. Each morning, as he had promised, Shimon would open the tractate chosen by Reuven at the beginning of the journey and father and son would study a page of Talmud together.

These journeys were often lonely. Reuven had spent his childhood in the cramped, smothering Jewish quarter of a minor town where everyone had known everyone else too well and nothing was hidden—there was an unavoidable intimacy with every neighbor that Reuven had taken for granted. But now there were strangers everywhere he turned, many of whom were not Jews, and Reuven felt the chill of isolation. He had panicked daydreams of his father falling ill or being trampled by a runaway horse, leaving him destitute, abandoned, and grieving. However, Shimon would soothe Reuven's nerves with kind words and taught his son how to speak more easily with strangers and distant acquaintances.

After two years of learning the wine trade, Reuven was ready for marriage. His father broached the matter to him after midnight prayers, back home, on a clear spring night. He said, Reuven, it is not good for a man to be alone. You are grown now, and it is time for you to take a wife. I have spoken with a matchmaker who has found a pious girl for you named Jael. She lives in Worms, not far away. Her father is in the wine trade, too—you met him when we were last in Tokay. He has promised you an excellent dowry and two years support in his house. They are coming here in three days. If you two are not averse to each other, it will be a match.

Count Raymond recalled again that first meeting with Jael. Terrified of the strange girl, he had wanted to shrivel to the size of a pebble and roll discreetly down the street. Yet when he finally worked up the courage to look at her he was relieved that she seemed equally frightened of him. They made stilted, awkward conversation—about the weather, about the wine trade. Jael showed him a blanket she had embroidered. The pattern was a fierce lioness protecting her cubs from a hunter dressed as a Christian. Why did you choose the lioness? he asked her.

To make me feel strong, she replied. I hope to have the strength to protect my litter against the wicked hunters someday.

And she giggled.

Jael and Melusine were such different creatures, he thought. Melusine was like one of those illustrations in the Christian Vulgate Bible manuscripts: more than humanly tall, slender, blonde, and pale; and she smelled only of flowers and fruits. Yet lovely as she was, Raymond had never felt entirely at ease when he touched her.

He could still summon the warm feel of Jael's calloused hands upon his skin. Sitting by a stove in wintertime, huddled together under a blanket, Jael had made her husband feel secure and loved in his nest.

The couple had been married in due course, and Reuven had gone to live with his new father-in-law in Worms. Now he made the nightly trek by himself for midnight prayers, where he would pray for a son who might—may he be so fortunate one day—follow him on a clear midnight to the riverbank. And those prayers were answered: Jael soon gave birth to Gershom, named for her grandfather of blessed memory.

Those were Reuven's happy years. His wine trading business did well, and he was able to build additions to his father-in-law's house in anticipation of a growing family. The sun seemed to shine brightly where he walked, and the shadows parted way for him, the merry man whose life was on the upswing.

His greatest joy was his son Gershom. When the boy was three years old, Reuven began to read stories to him from the Bible and the *Aggadah*, tales of the kings and judges of ancient Israel and their battles, and of the wise sages and their upright ways. Gershom especially loved the tale of how Rabbi Shimon ben Setah of blessed memory had tricked, captured, and vanquished eighty witches in Ashkelon so many years ago. Gershom demanded to hear this tale so often that Reuven's heart would sink when he was compelled to launch into it yet again. But nothing would deter his son when he was determined to hear his favorite story.

Part of the ritual of the storytelling was that Gershom would ask the same questions:

Tate, what is a witch?

She is a Gentile woman who worships idols and harnesses the power of demons.

Why are they bad? Why did the rabbi have to hurt them?

They use their powers for evil, to do bad things. The rabbi was protecting the Jews of Ashkelon.

But they don't do anything bad in the story. They just sit in their cave. So why did he think they would hurt people?

Because no one can employ such evil magic for good. If they had gone down that path, it must have been for a bad reason.

Sometimes that answer satisfied Gershom, or satisfied him enough as his eyelids weighed down in the fading candle-light. Still, other nights he would persist:

But *Tate*, what if one of the witches wanted to do good? Or was bad at first but changed her mind? Isn't that possible?

I guess it could be possible. The world has many wonders.

Then wasn't the rabbi wrong to punish the good witch along with the bad witches?

All witches are evil in the end. That kind of magic, that refusal to submit to the natural order decreed by the Holy One, Blessed be He, in His creation of the world, only leads to a wicked path. Sooner or later, no matter how good her intentions, her spells and potions lead to suffering because their source is polluted and profane and cannot be changed into anything else.

Count Raymond wondered if Gershom would have considered Melusine to be that elusive good witch who deserved a better fate than her sisters. Gershom—he could picture his round, pudgy face and hear that insistent singsong Yiddish questioning. With an effort he held back his tears.

Count Raymond reflected: When I was with Gershom he wore me down with his never-ending demands for this or that, and I yearned for five minutes peace and quiet. But when I traveled to buy and sell merchandise in other towns and lands, my heart was weighted down with so much sorrow because I was no longer with my son, and I longed for his voice again to harass me with a thousand tiny wishes.

He had been on one such journey when the terrible news reached him. It was a beautiful early summer day near the beginning of the Hebrew month of Sivan. Reuven was a three days' ride from his home in Worms, and he was inspecting barrels of wine for possible purchase. He had lingered to haggle back and forth with the vintner, sometimes inclining towards buying the wine, but then other times changing his mind.

Despite the warmth and light of the summertime, there were reasons to be unsettled, reasons which Reuven had largely not bothered to ponder. His Holiness Pope Urban II had recently called for a Crusade to liberate the Holy Land from Moslem rule, and in response marauding bands of knights had coalesced and begun to march towards Jerusalem. Some of the knights had been heard to say that it was time to wipe all Christ's enemies from the Earth, including their Savior's murderers, the wicked Jews, who lived spitefully amongst good Christians while they obstinately denied the gospel and slandered the Christian faith. One or two Jews had been beaten, perhaps seriously.

But none of this had disturbed Reuven. There were always bad Christians here or there, and the local lords and bishops would eventually bring them into line. Usually these men were debt-ridden drunkards more interested in extorting money from Jews than redeeming and converting souls. He trusted in the protection of the Christian lords, who had always been kind and loyal and had always maintained law and order.

Reuven's best customer in Worms was one such righteous Christian lord, Bishop Adalbert, the ruler of the small principality. Adalbert was a gentle old man, with deep lines in his face and thinning hair, and a smile that radiated both goodwill and a natural sense of command. The Bishop bought his wine primarily from Reuven, whom he would often ask about Jewish customs and practices.

Given his warm relations with the good Bishop, Reuven was not surprised when he was approached, on this same trip, by a servant from Adalbert's palace. They must be running low on wine, he thought, and want to see if I can broker a new purchase for their cellars. Yet when the servant sat down next to Reuven in the tavern, it was apparent that something was wrong. The man's clothes were disheveled, and his jittery eyes were jumping about the room. There was a gash across his left cheek. Although the man had walked straight up to Reuven, he could not look the wine merchant in the eye.

Heinrich, what troubles your soul? And how did you get that mark on your cheek? Here, rest, you are fine, the tavern keeper will bring us some mead—the local mead is surprisingly good here.

Heinrich heaved a piteous, woeful sigh, which sounded almost like a stifled sob. I am so sorry, he said, my lord the Bishop, he tried, he did, but he could not help. I am so sorry.

After draining a cup of mead to steady himself, Heinrich told his tale:

Count Emicho, a base man, well-known for his hatred of the Jews, had raised a company of knights to answer the Pope's call for a Crusade to liberate the Holy Land. But first, he insisted, his native Germany must be rid of the intolerable presence of the killers and original deniers of Christ, the wicked Jews. He and his band had terrorized the Jews they had found in the Rhineland.

In the month of May, according to the Christian calendar, Emicho and his knights had arrived in Worms, spreading lies about the Jews—that they had poisoned the well water, that they had murdered a Christian. The Bishop had tried to expose Emicho's lies, pointing out how the Jews had lived peacefully in Worms for many years and had helped the town to prosper through their trade. But it was all to no avail. Gangs of depraved men, their passions inflamed by these slanders, began to threaten the city's Jews. Bishop Adalbert had then ordered the Jews of Worms to take refuge in his palace, where he assured them they could safely wait out these disturbances.

Heinrich had seen both Jael and Gershom enter the palace courtyard. When he had asked where Reuven was, Jael had told him that her husband had journeyed to such-and-such town, which was how Heinrich later knew where to find him.

For eight days the palace fortifications held. Those were terrible days. The Jews wailed loudly and pitiably in their prayers when they did not bicker angrily amongst each other. From outside the walls Heinrich could hear the taunts and threats being shouted, and the banging on the gates with all sorts of weapons. Rocks were thrown up at the heads of the Bishop's sentries on the ramparts, who retreated from their posts in fear.

On the eighth day, the simmering mob broke through the gate and ransacked the palace. Heinrich had tried to fight back and received a deep cut to his face from some villain's dagger. It was confusion and screaming all around him. There were Jews plunging from the high windows of the keep to their deaths, and blood, blood everywhere, twisting and turning and burrowing into every stone and crevice.

Certain all the Jews were dead, Heinrich had fled here to tell Reuven of his wife and son's grim fates, and to warn him to stay away. Better yet, to flee the Rhineland, to get to safety in Normandy or Italy.

Reuven could not believe that Jael and Gershom had been murdered—how could this have happened on such a peaceful, sunlit day? Gentiles murdering all the Jews in their midst, who had heard of such things in the Rhineland? In the days of the distant past, of the Babylonians, of the Romans, certainly; but that was so long ago.

Groping for some reason to have hope, Reuven asked Heinrich if he had actually seen Jael and Gershom die.

Heinrich replied he had not, although he could not imagine how a woman and a tiny boy would have fought off dozens of armed knights.

But Reuven refused to despair—Heinrich could not be certain his family was not still alive somewhere. He decided to travel back to Worms to find them and bring them to a safe place. So he gathered his belongings, left word at the inn that he would return soon, and hired a cart and driver to take him home.

He did not sleep on the trip, although normally he would doze off from the rhythmic movements of the cart along the road. He told himself to pray, but he could not focus clearly enough to recall the right Hebrew words. He repeated the same few phrases in his mind: They can still be alive, do not grieve and do not weep.

The progress of the cart seemed painfully slow.

They were approaching a town where there was sure to be an inn. The driver said he needed to water the horses and to rest and eat himself.

Reuven was not pleased, but he could not argue with the coachman—the horses did need food and water to continue, and the driver needed to be alert enough not to crash the cart into a tree. So he grunted his approval.

At the inn Reuven ordered a glass of brandy to steady his nerves. Yet as he drank, he felt guilty—his Jael and Gershom were out there someplace, no doubt hurt, trembling in a muddy ditch, maybe feverish. And he was sitting in this inn enjoying a fine brandy. He explained to himself again that the horses needed oats and water, and that the driver needed sleep, that it would not help anyone if his cart fell into a ravine somewhere and he broke his legs. Still, he felt that he was in the wrong, in some indefinable way, simply for being there in the tavern and not in the ditch with his wife and son.

Suddenly there was a commotion in the inn. A hand grabbed him hard by the shoulder and pulled him up, knocking over the cup and the chair. Reuven, startled, looked up and saw the hand belonged to a knight in chainmail with a sword dangling from his waist. There were two other armed men next to him and a burgher from the town by their side.

Is this the Jew? One of the knights asked the burgher.

Yes, that is the Jew wine merchant.

Reuven now recognized the burgher: a rival wine merchant from the area.

The knight pushed Reuven forward. He tried to resist and break free, but another man unsheathed his sword and brought the sharp blade close to Reuven's neck. So he let the knights lead him away. The burgher meanwhile discretely melted away into the background.

They walked to the deserted town square, where he was led up the steps of the town's cathedral and inside to the baptismal font. There was an emaciated, acne-stricken young friar by the font, who looked at Reuven with angry eyes. The knight holding him adjusted his grip from Reuven's arm to his head, which he held over the water. Reuven saw the dead bodies of several men near his feet, whom he recognized as local Jews. Their glassy eyes were open and looking right through him. There were streaks of dried blood on the ground.

The friar called out: Jew, what is your name?

Reuven.

Jew Reuven, do you renounce the errors of your ways, your many crimes against Our Lord and Savior whom you betrayed and murdered, and accept holy baptism?

Reuven did not respond at first. So many images whirled in his mind—the corpses' empty staring eyes, Jael feeding Gershom at her breast, the river at midnight where his father had prayed. He tried to recall the words from his Hebrew prayer book, but he saw in his mind's eye the Hebrew letters jump from the page and run away from bands of Latin letters chasing them.

He felt a cold metallic sword-point rest lightly on his neck.

Answer us Jew. Salvation or death.

Hot urine dribbled down his thigh. Filled with a deep shame but unable to face death, he squeaked out: Baptism, baptism, baptism.

What is that Jew Reuven? Speak up.

Baptism, he said as loudly as he could.

He felt water splashing over his head as the friar rapidly recited Christian prayers in Latin. Reuven was convinced that it was his own urine that they had scooped up from a puddle on the ground and poured on his head, so polluted and defiled did he feel. He wanted to scrape his skin off his body and grow a new hide, like a shedding snake.

The knights soon left. Reuven slumped down in a corner, shaking and staring at the stone ground. When he looked up again, he saw that the friar had moved to the front of the church to perform some ritual at the altar. He stood up gingerly and walked towards the door.

He sat down outside on the cathedral steps. There was a small cross lying on the ground near him, which he figured someone must have accidently dropped. He picked it up and turned it around in his fingers. Then, in a sudden fit of rage, he threw the cross down and began to stomp upon it with his foot as hard as he could. A knight at the bottom of the steps saw him and rushed forward. Before Reuven could flee he had been cut to pieces.

Count Raymond sighed, and shed a solitary tear. The sun was now rising over the castle courtyard, and soon enough the priest would say morning mass in His Lordship's private chapel. His confessor would surely ask, gently of course, what disturbing thoughts had kept him from his rest at night—there were no doubt telltale rings under the Count's eyes. And what should the fine Christian lord Count Raymond, benefactor of so many local monasteries, say to his Christian priest? Who were the demons who had chased away his sleep, and what were his sins to confess?

IV. The Shame of the Noble Count

COUNT RAYMOND HAD been reading petitions from his vassals that day. One peasant claimed his neighbor had ruined his crops by permitting said neighbor's milk cow to graze upon his lands, while said neighbor in turn claimed that the original plaintiff had stolen his crops, and tried to slaughter his cow's newborn calf, to steal both the meat and the hide. Yet another petition begged for mercy and aid for a widow whose husband had suddenly fallen ill and died, leaving her with five small children to support. He learned from a third petition that a tavern-keeper was convinced that his stock of brandy was being stolen at night by mischievous, sinful youths. And on it went.

After an entire day devoted to reading these petitions, his eyes had grown sore, even though he had repeatedly dozed off for brief naps, from which he would awake with a start when he anxiously recalled the work that had to be done. Spending the day in the dusty library room, with the cold sun weakly penetrating the windows, left his limbs so heavy that they resisted any attempt he made to move them, although at the same time he yearned for nothing so much as a break from this penned-in monotonous grind.

A breathless, stammering servant girl at last came to his aid, telling him in hurried tones how the Lady Melusine had invited Lord Such-And-So and his traveling party to a banquet that night as her honored guests. Her Ladyship urgently requested His Lordship to dress for dinner. Raymond stretched and yawned and gladly shoved the pile of petitions to a corner of his desk.

At first the banquet cheered him. To Raymond's delight, Lord Such-And-So let loose his carefully curated stock of anecdotes and witticisms, although the visiting dignitary's companions were visibly bored at hearing these yet again. There were scandals of knights caught with chambermaids and a legend of a ghost haunting the countryside, who had apparently been summoned by an absentminded necromancer, who had forgotten to send the spirit back to its proper resting place. This ghost, thus stuck in the earthly realm, now delighted in making dramatic appearances in windows at night, but otherwise seemed to leave everyone well enough alone. Unfortunately, a peasant's wife had fallen madly in love with the specter, who she swore was the handsomest man she had ever beheld, and she wandered the meadows in the evening moaning after him.

Eventually the visiting lord grew tired of his tales, or noticed the glassy looks and gaping dumb jaws of his companions, and politely asked after Raymond and Melusine and their sons—where were the lads, anyway, they had already become such strapping fellows last time he had been in this area. Lord Such-And-So had looked forward to hunting with them, time permitting, of course.

Melusine clasped her hands together and smiled with pride. Our sons, she said, are not boys anymore. They are handsome, bold knights, and they have journeyed far away to prove their merit in battle. Both of our sons took the cross and traveled to the Holy Land to help reinforce King Baldwin's Crusader forces in Acre.

Lord Such-And-So appeared to be deeply moved. He recounted how his youngest son had also taken the cross and joined the original Crusade in 1096, but then had died in combat. A roadside shrine had been erected in his honor by some peasants, who were convinced that this fallen young knight had been almost a saint. After word of his martyrdom had reached home, a woman swore that the noble knight had come to her in a dream and promised to intercede with the heavenly powers to save her sick child in answer to her desperate prayers. The child, who was only two years old, then made an astonishing recovery from a crippling fever. Ever since that miracle the local peasants prayed to the martyred knight to plead with God on their behalf.

A servant in Lord Such-And-So's castle had found a chest of the young martyr's knickknacks—an old tunic, a hunting knife, a pelt, etc. These items, which the young man had not considered important enough to bring on his Crusade, now became holy relics in the roadside shrine. While the peasants had initially maintained the shrine, it had now been taken over by a group of local monks.

Melusine gushed forth praises for the fallen knight, and she was certain his pure holy soul watched over his family. She and her guests spoke eloquently about the bravery and nobility of the Crusaders, how they were willing to abandon their lands and families to sacrifice all in the cause of Christ.

Count Raymond said nothing. He burned with rage at each praise for the valor of the Crusaders, yet he was too terrified to speak. To let his thoughts show plainly would reveal him to be a fraud, an imposter, a filthy Jew playacting as a Christian lord. So he ground his teeth into his tongue until it bled. His silence and fear filled him with a terrible shame, as if he were an overgrown rat instead of a man.

The other members of Lord Such-And-So's party—a priest, a few knights, a coachman, a valet—now grew interested in the conversation and avidly filled in details about the fallen hero. He had not merely died in battle, but had ridden alone into a horde of Moslem knights when his fellow Crusaders had blanched with fear before the enemy's overwhelming numbers. And more: the night before his death Saint George had spoken to him in a dream, warning him that to go into battle the next day meant certain death, but that he would die as a holy martyr to Christ's true faith. There were rumors that, after a Moslem lance had finally penetrated his hauberk and laid him low, a kindly woman with sad eyes appeared from nowhere, lifted his corpse as if it were weightless and walked away with it to Paradise. Her grace and noble bearing had awed the unbelievers into mute submission.

Raymond doubled over with a horrible stomach cramp. There was a momentary pause in the conversation as his valet helped him to his feet and guided him back to his room. While he was being gently led away, he could hear the revelers start back up again, their voices rising with excitement.

Once he was alone, Raymond felt his body relax. He thought about his big, blond sons riding confidently in their armor through the Holy Land, trampling the ground where King David had first sung his psalms with heartfelt devotion to the Holy One, Blessed be He. Raymond imagined a scared little Moslem boy cowering in the shadow of his father, terrified and ashamed before the cruel, swaggering invaders. Raymond looked into the little boy's eyes and sobbed uncontrollably, as his whole body was flooded with wave after wave of grief for that imaginary child.

After he had tired himself out with sorrow, Raymond lay down on his bed and stared at the top of its canopy. Although the candles were sputtering out and no moonlight penetrated the curtains, his eyes would not close. He stared into the dark above him and felt the tracks of dried tears on his face.

This was how Melusine found him later that night. Placing her candle on a nearby table, she sat down on the edge of the bed and stroked his cheek.

Are you unwell? she asked.

I am better now.

Were you in pain? The servants heard your moans in the hallway.

Raymond took hold of her hand and removed it from his face. I grieved over unhappy memories, from before we met.

Melusine sighed and clasped her hands in her lap. Raymond, dear, it is not good to think of the times from before we met. None of that is real anymore. You were born anew, better, as my bridegroom. As I have told you so many times, we should not discuss past wounds.

Her words brought to mind the many times he had tried to broach his past with her. He had not dared to discuss his old life with anyone else, lest he be exposed as a sham Christian and a sham nobleman, but Melusine at least knew something of the truth—she had found his severed body parts, so she must have known there was something terrible that had come before her. Yet each time he had mentioned the past to try to share some of his tender grief for Jael and Gershom, she gently scolded him and smothered his mouth with her soft lips.

But on this night, when Melusine reached down to kiss his sorrows away, something in her breath made him turn away. The lavender scents she emitted seemed less a comfort this time than a trap, although for what he could not have said.

Raymond, you truly are sad this evening. Yet we had such lovely company. And you see the esteem in which our sons are held, how they are admired for their chivalry and bravery. Come to me, I can take away all the suffering.

Raymond sat up and pushed her away. He took a deep breath, but felt the air in the room was stifling. Without further word, he walked away. She called out, but when he did not respond, she did not get up to follow him. He walked through the dimly lit castle corridors, declining the servants' offers of aid. He had at first thought he would take a walk outside and inhale some fresh air, but he had somehow forgotten how to exit his own castle. He went down one hallway, and then another, and looped back again and around, but seemed trapped in an endless circle.

Exhausted and feverish, he slumped down against a wall in a dark hallway and let his head rest against a jutting stone.

He breathed deeply again. The air smelled awful, and he realized he was not far from a privy. I am trapped in my defilement, he thought, as he finally slipped into a deep slumber.

Raymond awoke back in his room, with Melusine sitting once more on the edge of the bed. The sun beamed in brightly through the window.

I am glad you are awake again, she said. Lord Such-And-So and his party have departed. The servants found you lying on the ground outside a privy. You were clearly quite ill last night. But the color has returned to your face, and you seem better now. My kiss will finish healing you. Tell me you love me, and I will give you a healing kiss that will send your soul spinning with delight.

Raymond demurred. He was still not well, he told her. He needed to eat.

Yet even after eating, Raymond avoided Lady Melusine. He busied himself with petitions, Bible studies, inspections of the vineyards, even hearing Mass multiple times each day. Days and then weeks passed in this fashion: He would work himself to exhaustion so he could collapse right after his evening meal into a numb sleep and thereby elude his wife's caresses.

Melusine's eyes struck him as increasingly filled with anxiety. She took to wearing her most flattering dresses and letting her long yellow hair cascade flirtatiously down her shoulders. Raymond stared at her across tables and halls and told himself he should be thankful for such an extraordinary wife. Yet he felt nothing but disgust. She seemed to him to be subtly but thoroughly caked in a film of some awful, impure substance, and he was sure her kiss would contaminate him with this toxic element. He was grateful now for Saturdays when, as always, she would seclude herself all day.

One night she woke him after he had gone early to bed. Raymond sat up and rubbed the sleep from his eyes. She had placed a candle on a table near the bed, and he could see there were tears falling down from her bloodshot eyes.

He knew he had treated her cruelly. But when he looked closely at her face, with her light blond coloring, he was struck by the resemblance between her and her sons, those sons bearing the cross for the Crusader Kingdom in the Holy Land.

Melusine broke the silence: It has been many weeks since you last swore your love to me. I cannot go on without hearing you pledge your love. Please tell me, again, that you love me and will love me forevermore.

But I have told you many times before, he replied, why do you need to hear it again? I am tired, I am working so hard to administer our domains.

Melusine moaned. Why can't you see how important your love is? Just speak the words. Let me kiss you again.

Raymond could not bring himself to show her the kindness for which she begged. He closed his eyes again to avoid looking further into his wife's sad countenance, which seemed both a condemnation of his callousness and a lure into betrayal of something else. He felt polluted, as if he needed to escape his fairy queen and her enchantments to purify himself.

V. The Gifts of the Prophet Elijah

AFTER A TIRING trek through the forests and roads just outside his domains, Count Raymond had found the shrine to the martyred Crusader son of Lord Such-And-So. He had felt driven to confront the ghost of the slain knight, to denounce him as a criminal hypocrite, but when he finally reached the shrine he had to stifle his laughter: there, upon a grandiloquent marble altar —a gift from the lordly father, no doubt—and flanked by statuettes of angels, were the holy martyr's sacred relics, which included broken combs, torn underpants stained with brownish splotches, and a cracked blue bottle stinking of some rancid medicine. His acolytes had apparently been compelled to ransack his childhood rooms, as the Moslem knights who had overpowered him had no doubt taken his arms and more noble belongings for themselves. Despite the absurdity of these relics, two stern friars stood guard over the altar, demanding donations before the peasants were permitted to beseech the martyr's aid.

The crowd about the shrine fell silent when they noticed Raymond. The monks bowed their heads and thanked His

Lordship for honoring their humble reliquary with a visit. They praised Raymond as himself the father of two brave Crusader knights and asked if he would like to beseech the martyred knight to bless and watch over his children fighting for Christ in the Holy Land.

Raymond assumed a solemn air and thanked the brothers for their kind words. He asked for a private moment with the relics, so he could offer his prayers to the martyr's soul in Heaven. The monks cleared the crowd away and left him alone next to the altar.

Raymond clasped his hands together in a gesture of prayer and leaned forward. His eyes alighted once more on the brown spots in the old underpants. He moved closer to the shrine and elevated himself by stepping on a large stone lying next to it, so that his waist was now level with the relics. On a sudden whim, he lifted his robe slightly and aimed a drizzle of urine upon the sacred relics. He grinned when he saw his newly spread drops glisten in the sun. There, he thought, a fitting prayer for my sons, the gallant and chivalrous Crusaders. For a moment, the heaviness lifted from his heart and his spirit soared gloriously in the clouds.

But then panic seized Raymond: What if someone had seen his insulting gesture? The people, the Church, certainly Lord Such-And-So, would descend upon him with holy wrath. Perhaps questions would again be raised about his background, and they would see him finally as the absurd fraud that he was.

He jumped off the stone and fled from the shrine. No one seemed to be around, but he could not be certain. He walked quickly back to the main road, where he had left his servants.

They praised him for having sought the protection of the holy martyr for his sons risking their lives to protect the honor of Christendom. Raymond nodded, thanked them for their fine words, and sent them back to the castle. He promised to follow shortly, but he said he needed more time alone with his thoughts and prayers.

He wandered far from the shrine and the road, deep into the forest. The din of human sounds faded away until he was hemmed in by the forest's dark stillness. His feet meandered aimlessly around tree after tree and bush after bush, while his mind emptied and his muscles relaxed. Time and distance dissolved. He was Adam in the Garden of Eden now, before there was an Eve, drifting among the plants and animals in an existence with no past and no future, no childhood and no old age, just an endless idyll under the canopies of green leaves far above his head.

As the day wore on, the weak light peeking through those high leaves faded and then turned purple. Under the twilight, new human sounds startled Raymond out of his reverie. The sounds were muffled and indistinct, but his feet were drawn to them and, as he approached, he could make out two voices chanting. The words were not German or Latin, but he knew them somehow. The chanting warmed his soul and he felt like a small boy again in his father's lap, nestling his nose into that soft belly and feeling the rough skin of his father's palm upon his cheek.

He began to chant too, soon quite loudly. The words flowed out of him, as if they had been bottled up too long in a corner of his throat and needed to be released. Raymond realized these words were Hebrew, and he recognized them as the prayers with which his father had greeted the holy Sabbath on Friday evenings.

The other two men stopped their chanting and walked over to him. They were young, probably, he guessed, the same age as his Crusader sons.

My good Jew, one of them began, I see you are also stranded in the forest for the Sabbath. Will you pray with us? We have food, not much, but it will sustain us until the end of the holiday, when we can resume our journey and find our way home. What is your name?

Reuven.

Reb Reuven, why are you dressed up like some Christian nobleman? And where are your *tzitzit*? You look like you are playing King Ahasuerus in a Purim play.

I was bathing by a river when my clothes were stolen. I ran ashamed through the forest until I came upon these clothes and put them on. I think I make a fine Christian lord. Perhaps I will keep them.

The two young Jews laughed and resumed their prayers, now accompanied by Reuven. Night fell and by the dim starlight peeking through the treetops the three men shared a Sabbath meal of black bread and pickled herring. Reuven felt that, for the first time in years, he could actually taste his food, as it was not secreted away beneath the overpowering spices and sauces conjured by the castle cook.

Once the meal was completed, the three men huddled together at the foot of a wide tree trunk. After perhaps a quarter of an hour or so (Reuven could not easily tell how much time had passed), a light appeared between the branches in the distance, a bright silver glowing ball. The silver light steadily came closer and grew larger, until it was right in front of them. The three good Jews averted their eyes from the blinding glare, but when they nervously looked up again, they beheld a short, friendly old man with a bushy beard and a well-carved walking stick.

The man looked down at them and laughed: Three fine Jews choose to spend the holy *Shabbat* in the forest with the boars and the wolves, and it is me that scares them.

The old man paused for a few moments, but the three Jews continued to cower in silence.

Well, I suppose you are hungry. I do not live far from here, and I have the most wonderful goose meat and honey cakes upon my table. Come, get up, let me merit the *mitzvah* of showing kindness and hospitality to strangers. We were all once strangers in a strange land and we know the heart of the stranger.

Reuven had begun to feel a chill in the air, and he thought the old man had a point about the wild animals. So he stood up first, and then his younger companions followed. The three trailed behind the old man's silver light—which seemed to glow from his walking stick—through the trees and bushes until they reached the side of a mountain.

The old man led them into a cave, where his glowing staff was the only light. There was just enough space for each man to stand and spread his arms out. Deeper into the Earth they walked until there were no more sounds reaching them from the surface. Reuven was terrified of this dark, isolated place, but he decided to see this adventure through—there was something reassuring about the old man's kindly demeanor.

The ground leveled out and the old man told his guests not to lose heart, they were almost there. Reuven soon felt his feet moving upward again on a steep incline. The old man quickened his pace, forcing his three companions to follow suit, even though they begged him to slow down. The light went out in the staff, but, after a brief moment of alarm in the pitch dark, the group came safely out the other side into a large garden.

It was twilight in this garden, with a dim sliver of a moon hanging in the pink firmament. The weather was mild, with a light, massaging breeze. Reuven was astounded by the beautiful, peaceful scene: The flowers were in bloom, the trees were filled with ripe fruits of many colors, and the birds sang sweet melancholy songs of longing and resignation.

The old man led them to a clearing in which there was a villa. This building did not resemble the castles and battlements of the bellicose Christian lords of the European countryside. It had a wide portico with tall white marble columns, but no defensive moats or ramparts or gates. When they entered Reuven beheld a brightly lit, cavernous hall made, again, of white marble. The old man invited his guests to sit at the table in the middle of the hall.

The others will be coming soon, the old man said before disappearing into a far corner. And soon enough, other guests came. These other guests wore dazzling green and blue robes and, like the old man, carried walking sticks that glowed with different colors. One of these new guests sat next to Reuven. His face was strikingly handsome.

The old man returned and set the table, laying out pitchers of sweet-smelling wine and mead, heaps of goose meat and fish, and trays of honey cakes. When he was finished, the old man gestured to the guest who had sat down next to Reuven. This fine-looking man stood and sang the *kiddush* prayer with such passion that Reuven felt carried away by the Hebrew words and melody.

That *Shabbat* meal was the finest Reuven had ever tasted—neither Melusine's magic nor the wealth of any Christian nobleman could summon such wondrous delicacies. With each bite to eat and draught to drink, Reuven felt something inside his body heal, some little festering sore in the back of his throat or sore muscle in his leg. A sense of calm and belonging washed over him.

He asked his companion what his name was and how he had come to this place.

I am Joseph, the man said, I came here from Egypt, where I had lived out my days in glory by the Pharaoh's side. When my life reached its end, the Holy One, Blessed be He, brought me here where I have dwelled ever since.

Who is the old man who brought us here?

Joseph smiled slyly. You did not recognize him? Whom does the Holy One send when poor Jews are alone, abandoned and in need? Think upon the matter—you know who he is as sure as you are a Jew.

But I am not a poor Jew, Reuven replied. That is, well, I may be a Jew—or I may not—but I am not poor. I am a wealthy lord. I have a palace, lands that I rule, servants, vassals, knights, and a wife with loveliness and enchantments that are beyond human.

Joseph laughed. You are a Jew and you are poor. Did you inherit these lands? Conquer them? Your wife is a demon who has spun illusions for your eyes. She uses you, yet you are too foolish to see. All the worldly adornments she has draped upon you will blow away like chaff in the wind, revealing the wretched shivering poor Jew beneath them.

But tonight ... tonight you have been blessed. Elijah the Prophet does not usually see fit to bring his guests all the way here. He often settles for conjuring a hut in a forest with a warm hearth and freshly baked bread. He must have felt one of you, or all of you, needed the special healing that only this place can bring. This garden is a land of eternal bloom and youth, where the Earth is always in that first, happy burst of bliss at the miracle of existence.

Reuven drank another glass of mead and looked around the table. Except for himself and his two original companions, all the guests had translucent skin and floated in the air like phantoms, although their faces were radiant and their beards and eyes black and shining.

And then a thought troubled him: Where was Melusine? With all her magical powers, surely she could have found this place and joined him. Or taken him home. So he asked Joseph: Can my wife Melusine see us here? Can she journey to this place?

He shook his head. No, she cannot enter here. I told you she is a demon, a deceiver, and this is a place of holiness and sanctity. She had wanted to defile you thoroughly, but your Jewish soul survived, otherwise you could never have set foot in this garden. The food and drink from this table will heal you from her wounds and wash away the sticky threads of her web—that must be why you were brought here—and when you return to your demon bride, your eyes will see differently.

But enough words. When it is your soul's time, you will return here again, and you will be able to study these things and more at the feet of the wisest sages who have ever lived.

Until then …

Reuven watched the room fade to a blur, and the murmuring of the voices grew distant. He stood up and staggered several steps before his knees buckled and his body pounded into the hard marble ground. Elijah knelt down beside him and spoke words of comfort.

You have tasted the delights of the Garden of Eden, but any more will overwhelm you—your flesh is too weak for such holiness except in small portions. But you have received what you needed to heal your wounds and to restore your true sight. The *Shabbat* has ended—time moves at a different pace here— and you must return to the profane world of the week.

Elijah cradled Reuven's head in his two palms, leaned down, and kissed his forehead. Reuven fell into a deep sleep.

VI. With Sight Restored

COUNT RAYMOND WAS gently shaken awake by his castle steward. After rubbing the sleep from his eyes, he saw that he was lying between a tree trunk and the old Roman highway running through the forest. His steward was flanked by several knights and pages.

My Lord, praise be to God that we found you. The Lady Melusine was beside herself with worry when you did not return to the castle, and she dispatched us at dawn to search for you. Come, my Lord, we will be home soon.

Although he had slept on the hard ground against the jutting tree roots, Raymond felt remarkably well rested. His body was soft and unblemished, as if, he thought, he had just emerged a freshly baked loaf from the oven. When he arrived at the castle courtyard Melusine threw her arms around his neck and muttered prayers of thanksgiving.

Yet her touch felt heavy and oppressive. Raymond stood back and looked searchingly at his wife. For the first time since they had met, she struck him as no longer beautiful.

Not ugly, he thought, just not beautiful anymore. This puzzled him because her figure and her features were the same. But somehow the glow from within her had faded away. Her eyes seemed almost glassy. And her skin seemed somehow artificial, more like an expensive dress than true human skin.

Wishing to be rid of her, Raymond stiffly thanked Melusine for her warm greetings and her thoughtfulness in dispatching the search party after he had unfortunately become lost in the forest, but—praise be to God!—he had come out fine from his mishap. Now, however, he had to return to his petitions and to his tax records, which he had meant to address yesterday, before he had been waylaid.

Melusine appeared confused and worried by this response. Needing some way to break the impasse and get away from her, he patted her shoulder, and walked into the castle to his study.

After he had been hard at work for an hour or so, Lady Melusine entered his study and sat down. Out of politeness, Raymond put his papers down and turned to face her. She had that same anxiety in her eyes.

Raymond, she began, I fear for you. Last night, despite summoning all my special abilities, I could not see you. I worry you have fallen under a dark spell, that some evil sorcerer or jealous fairy captured you and twisted your sight. The way you look at me now, it is with so little love. You must tell me what happened, so I can help you. I can remove the sand from your eyes and the stones from your heart, and we can love each other as before.

Melusine's words brought Joseph's comments back to his mind—how his wife was a demon, how her dark vision could not penetrate the holy walls of the Garden of Eden. Still, what if Melusine was right? What if that had not been Elijah, but a malicious forest fairy who had deceived him? But he had felt so at home in the Garden, hearing the Hebrew chanting—like he was a boy again in his father's lap in the synagogue—and how could an evil sprite have created such holiness? Wasn't it the way of such wicked spirits to tempt with sin, with lust, or greed?

Feeling uncertain, Raymond chose to conceal what had happened.

I became lost in the forest and fell asleep. A bit embarrassing, but there were no enchantments.

Please don't lie to me, Melusine said. Something happened. Our love is precious and has created this beautiful life—these lands and this castle, our heroic and noble sons doing great deeds in the Holy Land. If you betray my love and trust, it will all vanish. Whatever you saw, whatever you heard, it was not real, it was trickery, deception. This is your truth, here, you and I bound together in love.

Raymond reflected that he should be moved by her words—that would be the appropriate response, and he had been deeply moved by far less intense pleas in the past. Yet her words now left him cold. What if it all vanished? What was this anyway, this absurd life where a poor Jew pretends to be a mighty Christian lord? Was this not trickery and deception on the grandest scale?

So Raymond held his ground: There is nothing more to tell. I still love you as much as ever. I do not mean to be unkind, but I lost too much time yesterday and my duties are pressing. This life we have built includes many obligations.

Melusine quietly left the room. Shortly afterwards, in the distance down the hallway, he could hear muffled sobs.

Dreading another confrontation, Raymond set out on a journey for several weeks to inspect his vineyards and to visit the bishop, with whom he had business affairs to settle. Nevertheless, certain gossip trickled back to him as he made his rounds of the countryside. It was said that Melusine had been unable to sleep. She had been seen to mount the top of the highest castle tower in the midnight hour, where she would invoke horrible spells with her features twisted unnaturally in the moonlight. Some servants swore she had sprouted wings and horns.

By day she appeared to look right through people. Or she would be composed, her usual noble self, when suddenly something would catch her eye in the distance—no one knew what—and she would scream in terror, as if Lucifer himself had bared his hideous features to her.

There was also talk of what had really happened to the noble Count Raymond in the forest. Some loose tongues insisted that he had been attempting to escape her clutches, maybe even to travel to—or at least get word to—his sons in the Holy Land to tell them that his wife, their mother, had entered into a diabolical pact with the Devil. Others claimed that she had lured him into the forest for a witches' Sabbath, for some debauched ritual with demonic powers, but that something had gone awry. Or maybe it was Raymond who had led his wife to sin—he had, after all, risen from ignoble birth to noble status, perhaps he had even greater ambitions now and had turned to Satan in his thirst for power and wealth. Or had the Devil seduced them both?

Raymond was troubled by what he heard. He knew so little about his wife, despite all their years together. He had sometimes asked about her past before him, or from what source she drew for her extraordinary magic. But Melusine would put her finger on his lips and say that these were not things worth dwelling upon—neither of them should speak of past things, they had been reborn into a new, better life, and should not spoil it. The only truth, she would say, is what you see and feel and hear right now, my love, not the phantoms who try to haunt your sleep or mine. For a long time, her words had melted his worries away—or at least so he had thought. Everything now was such a jumble: fairy or demon? Blessing or curse?

Raymond grew suspicious of Melusine's secret, isolated Saturdays. To be left alone on Saturday had been Melusine's one and only condition for their wedded bliss, and he had seen no reason not to agree. He had supposed that everyone now and then could use some time to be alone with one's thoughts and prayers, the way he used to pray alone at midnight. And he had always kept his vow to stay away on these Saturdays. But now he wondered: What was she doing all alone? Was this when she communed with dark spirits? Or reported back to them on her progress in fulfilling their infernal wishes?

Raymond reviewed what he knew about her Saturday escapes. Melusine would wake early, dress hurriedly, and speak to no one. She would descend into the castle cellar, rush past the wine barrels, past the barley sacks, through the maze of broken furnishings that had been left to rot down there, and, finding yet another staircase, descend into a chamber deep within the bowels of the Earth. There she would spend her

Saturdays. Guards were posted at the point where the barley sacks met the busted remains of old chairs and chandeliers—and upon pain of death, no one but the Lady Melusine could go past them on a Saturday.

At the stroke of midnight when Saturday became Sunday, Melusine would emerge from this subterranean lair and lightly, gleefully, dance up the castle stairways and hallways until she had reached Raymond's bed. She would pounce upon him like a frisky cat, and kiss him and embrace him and declare her everlasting love. In that borderland between dreaming and waking in the middle of the night, she would appear to Raymond as an angel sent from Paradise, the most lovely and the most love-worthy of all creatures.

When Raymond completed his tour of his estates and returned again to the castle, he was resolved to know the truth of the magic that had elevated him from dismembered Jewish corpse to illustrious Christian lord.

VII. Raymond's Betrayal

I KNOW YOU are there, in the corner, I know you have betrayed me. Stand up, come forward, see what you wanted to see. Dank corners are not fitting places for great lords like my noble husband.

So spoke the Lady Melusine to her husband, Count Raymond, in the early morning hours of a Saturday, as he lay crouched, hidden he had believed, behind a pile of broken stones in that underground room where she spent her solitary Saturdays. Raymond had surreptitiously left his bed the previous night and burrowed into this hiding place, waiting for his wife to come, desperate as he was to learn her secret.

And came she did and submerged herself in a wide stone tub. In the dim light from the torches on the walls, he could see steam rise as Melusine let all of her body below her chin slip into the boiling hot bath. She stifled a sob, as if her body was afflicted with sudden shooting pains, but then sighed with relief and closed her eyes. Raymond lost track of time as he watched from his corner.

When she opened her eyes again, she called out to her husband to leave his ignoble hiding place and stand before her openly. He mutely obeyed, although he felt ashamed at having broken his vow.

Look down into the tub, she instructed, see what you came to see.

Raymond obeyed again. But what he saw made him freeze in terror: From the waist down, Melusine had become a gigantic, writhing green-and-black snake.

What are you? he asked. Are you a demon? Is this all dark, evil magic—all of it, the castle, the lands, our sons, all of it demon trickery?

A trickle of quiet tears rolled down Melusine's pale face. No, Raymond, I am not a demon. I blessed you with my love, and now you have betrayed me.

You are not human. What else can you be but a demon? A daughter of foul Lilith? Why have you tempted me, attacked me? Why could you not have let my soul ascend to the World to Come to join my Jael and my Gershom?

She gazed at him with eyes expressing such disappointment. Why must you know these things, my love? We can live beautifully, if only we give ourselves fully to the dream that I have made real. We did not exist before we met—everything before was illusion, deception—and everything after is true. If you insist that what came before has to be real, then this dream will wither away. There is a price to knowing. Once you know, you cannot be the same Raymond any longer.

He hesitated. There was a pleading look in his wife's eyes, which filled him with tenderness—perhaps she was trying to help him? Was his life so awful floating in her soft embrace?

But no: These could be the demon's tricks. He had to learn the truth of the matter.

Tell me. And I am not your Raymond. I am Reuven, son of Shimon, husband of Jael.

Melusine's face narrowed in rage and her snake tail rustled angrily in the water. A hissing sound escaped her lips. He wanted to move away, but felt paralyzed.

If you want to know, then you shall know, betrayer, wretch. But you will not move again until I have shown you everything you must see to know me and to know yourself. You will be cursed forevermore for this decision of yours about what is real and what is illusion.

Raymond could no longer feel his body. He was not sure if he was still breathing. But his eyes could see and his ears could hear.

Melusine breathed deeply and began:

In one of the islands in the far north of the world, in a land beyond where the Jews have roamed in their exile, there was a king named Elynas. He was young, handsome, brave, the greatest warrior and the keenest hunter in those wild, frozen northern lands. He had his choice of princesses to wed, but Elynas was too arrogant to settle for a human bride, who would be destined to grow old and whose beauty would fade. He longed for a fairy, a creature with the magic to be eternally young and lovely for him all of his days.

So he wandered the crags and the forests, killing and roasting wolves and boars as he went. One day he came to a spring, where the water tasted sweet and warmed his shivering bones. He heard singing nearby, sad songs in a strange tongue, and he followed the sounds down the bank until he came upon the lovely Pressyne sitting upon a marble throne in the grass, facing the water and all its creatures.

Elynas knew immediately that she was the enchanted fay for whom he had longed. He fell to his knees before her and swore his eternal love. He pledged to devote all his strength and riches to her happiness, if only she would marry him.

Pressyne gently told him it could not be, for how could an immortal fairy wed a man who would die? His life would be a flicker in her eye, leaving her to mourn him for the rest of time. How could he wish such a fate upon her, if he truly wanted her to be happy? A handsome, powerful man like him could bring so much joy to a human woman, and that would be more fitting.

But Elynas would not desist. He grabbed her by the ankles, and he moaned and pleaded and begged. Eventually he wore away Pressyne's resistance. And she later admitted to me that *his* great beauty, his broad back and thick muscles and blond locks, had flooded her with desire. So Pressyne agreed to marry Elynas, but she made him swear never to set eyes upon her at certain times, including childbirth. Overjoyed, Elynas agreed to whatever she asked without paying any attention to the promises he was making. The two lovers mounted his horse together, and they rode to his castle to celebrate the wedding.

Soon Pressyne was pregnant. When it came time for her to give birth, she went, alone, into a tent pitched beyond the castle walls and warned Elynas not to look upon her again until she should choose to return to him.

At first Elynas obeyed, although, so great was his desire to see his beautiful fairy bride, he could not bring himself to wander far from that tent. Fairy women do not give birth the way human women do. There is no pain, or blood, or suffering. Instead it is a calm, joyous experience. The mother swoons with delight as she imparts magical gifts to her children slowly exiting from her womb.

But Pressyne had not warned her husband that fairy births are peaceful. He had expected screams of horrible agony, yet all he could hear were owls hooting indifferently in the nearby trees. Elynas was terrified that something had gone horribly wrong and could barely keep himself away. Then, delirious with happiness at the dawn of new life, Pressyne broke out in rapturous song. Her clear, crystal voice reached out to her husband's ears and soothed his worried heart. Soothed it too much, alas: Carried away by the beauty of the song, he could no longer bear to be away from such a perfect, enchanted being.

He burst into the tent just as Pressyne gave birth to three daughters—one of whom was me. Her song stopped abruptly, and she sharply rebuked him for breaking his promise. Pressyne swore that, as a fitting punishment, he could no longer gaze upon her face or hear her song.

You must understand that fairies can only give gifts to humans—including the gift of love—in exchange for some promise or condition that must be followed without the slightest deviation. That is just how fairy magic works. Even though Elynas pleaded that he had had the best of intentions and Pressyne believed him, she still had no choice but to withdraw her gifts. So she gathered up her newborn daughters in her arms, spread her wings, and flew away to Avalon, the island of the fairies.

I grew up with my sisters in Avalon. The weather was always warm, and the rain, which fell only so often, tasted like honey on your tongue. Everywhere there were trees bursting with the most delicious fruit, which was immediately replenished as soon it was picked. The island was filled with small birds hopping and singing, and bees that made the flowers bloom, but no dangerous animals—no wolves, no bears.

Yet perfect as it all was, I felt incomplete. I would sit on the beach and watch the sea and yearn for something indescribable and far away. My sisters felt the same way. The other fairies on the island were content singing and playing games in their paradise, but not us three.

One day, when we had grown from girls to women, our mother told us that we were not like the other fairies. We were half-human, and that strange longing inside us was a budding human soul. Fairies have no souls, you see, fairies cannot shed their bodies and transcend this world to enter the higher realms. But humans can. That is why fairies have eternal youth, never losing their charms to age, but human bodies wither and rot so the immortal soul can shed the bodily prison of loathsome flesh and rise up to Heaven.

So if we are partly human, we asked, where is our father? We want to see him. We want him to show us how to use our souls, how to ascend someday to Heaven, too, with him. At these words, our mother burst into tears and told us, between sobs and moans, how she had loved Elynas and how he had betrayed her.

I was filled with rage. How could our father be so callous? So selfish? I wanted to be held and rocked by my father, to feel the warmth of his love—that, I somehow knew, was what my budding soul needed to grow. Yet he had driven our mother away and so deprived us of his fatherly love. I blamed my restless yearning upon him—he had not been the father he should have been to us, he had left us to twist in confusion amid the oblivious frolicsome fairies, who did not know how a soul's longings could torment you day and night.

I made up my mind to get revenge on our father, Elynas. My sisters and I secretly conjured a boat from the depths of the sea, which we commanded to take us to his land. When we disembarked, we were horrified by the desolation of the place. It was winter, and the winds lashed at our delicate, exposed skin. The trees had no fruit or flowers or leaves. The snow banks surrounded us, penning us in, and each time we slipped and fell the dense packed snow bruised our bones.

We trudged on until we came to a campsite. There he was, our father, with his men. How did we know it was him? We just did—our budding souls were reaching out for the reassuring warmth of his grizzled palm. He was no longer young, but not yet old, and still muscular and handsome. The men in the camp showed him great honor. There were piles of dead animals—great stags—heaped up near the fires.

That night, after the men had fallen asleep, we went to our father's tent and sang so softly that only he could hear our lovely fairy song. His eyes burst open and welled up with tears of longing and regret. We moved back and he followed us, followed our song. We lured him to the edge of a cave, and then threw him down a pit into the belly of the mountain. We cast a spell to seal the cave.

Our triumph was brief. My mother had grown suspicious and traced us to that very mountain—for fairy magic is dogged—where she rebuked us sternly. Our father had never betrayed us, she said, and she had already punished him for wronging her. Pressyne freed Elynas and restored him to his tent.

Then she cursed each of us. We were henceforth exiled from Avalon and from each other. We were cursed to become deformed monsters every Saturday. However, while we could not return to Avalon or be whole in our beauty, she told us that we could save ourselves the human way: by saving our souls. If we could find a human man to love us and not betray us, then his soul's love would repair and gird our souls, which, when they had grown strong enough, would break free from our bodies and join our beloveds in Heaven.

My mother dropped me at the northernmost point of the Rhine River. I wandered down the river, sometimes by foot on the bank, sometimes swimming. I thought about how to find a man whose love would redeem my soul. My mother's experience was a cautionary tale. It is easy for a fairy to use her beauty and her song to seduce a human man's heart, and I could have fetched a handsome, muscular lord like my father. But such a man, I realized, would see me as a trophy, another mighty boar felled by his spear. He would make me one of his things to be displayed, but what he displayed—pelts, swords, halls—lacked souls and could be carelessly damaged or discarded in a drunken escapade. No, I needed a lowly man to lift up and bless, who would feel such gratitude for my gifts to him that he could not fail but to love me in return, forevermore.

Down the Rhine I went, and I soon saw certain men being persecuted by other men. The men being hounded, I learned, were Jews. I sang out to these Jewish men and offered to save them in exchange for their love. But they scorned me and reviled me as a demon, a wanton and immoral daughter of Lilith. They killed themselves and each other rather than be captured by their pursuers, claiming to be sacrifices to God— to die for the unity and sanctification of His Holy Name. I could not understand their eagerness to die rather than fall to safety in my arms. They found me beautiful, I could see that in their hungry stares, but somehow my beauty terrified and repulsed them, and made them redouble their efforts to plunge into death.

Then I found you, a Jew cut into pieces. I decided to take a chance: If I put you together again and brought you back to life, would you then be grateful and love me?

And it worked. I patched you up, and you loved me. I lifted you to heights beyond the dreams of any Jew. I gave you sons, new sons, better sons. I transformed your seed in my womb to make our sons beautiful and tall and strong, great heroes and knights, not trembling sickly Jews squinting over their old books. I gave you perfect happiness.

Yet you still betrayed me. Something—someone—came between us. You have hidden it from me, but what does that matter? Your foul betrayal has come to pass and that cannot be undone now.

VIII. The Truth of the Matter

AND NOW, MELUSINE continued, I will curse you for betraying my love. Look into this pool of water, and you will see the truth of your fate, from which I have shielded you in my wondrous, sweet fog.

Raymond felt an irresistible force move his neck, face, and eyes so he was forced to gaze into the dead center of the tub, right above where Melusine's serpent's tail swished back and forth. A black circle formed upon the surface of the water and then an image began to form inside the circle.

There was Bishop Adalbert's palace courtyard in Worms. The gates were opening. The Bishop's men, mounted and armed, were escorting the town's Jews inside. Raymond saw Jael, holding Gershom's small hand. He had clearly been crying, and his limbs shook with fear. Raymond heard Jael comforting Gershom, telling him they would be safe here from the wicked men. The Bishop, she continued, was a righteous man who had promised to keep them safe. The wicked men will leave, *Tate* will come home, and I will cook you both the most delicious *kugel*.

The circle faded to black again before another image formed. It was the great hall in Adalbert's palace, with its vaulted windows, which was filled with Worms' Jews. There were sounds, screams and shouts and banging metal, in the distance. A man rushed into the room—a Jew, who looked familiar, but Raymond could not place him—and this man told the crowd of other Jews that Count Emicho, his Crusader knights, and the angry mob of burghers had breached the gates of the castle. The courage of the Bishop's men was faltering, and they were abandoning their posts rather than be cut down by the overwhelming force of the invaders. The Bishop was urging the Jews to submit to baptism to save their lives, as Emicho had sworn to spare the life of any Jew who renounced the Jewish faith and accepted Christianity.

The Jews debated what to do. There was no escape except to plunge to their deaths from the other side of the ramparts. Several men, distinguished merchants, contended that baptism would be the best option. They pointed out that the Torah teaches that the Holy One, Blessed be He, had set before Israel both life and death, and commanded His people to choose life so that they and their children may live.

And, these prudent men continued, what happens after we are baptized? The wicked Crusaders will go on their way to fight the Moslems in the Holy Land. The Bishop will nullify the conversions as being made under duress and not of our free will. If the Bishop tries to enforce the baptisms, we will simply pack our belongings and wander until we find a lord who recognizes that we are still Jews. There are many lords who can offer aid and protection, and we need to find only one upright man among them. Baptism will save our lives now, so we can continue Israel's seed on this Earth, but be of no consequence in a month's time. Let us be sensible and remember there will be many more days yet to come.

There were murmurs of approval until Jael, holding Gershom, demanded to speak. All eyes in the hall turned towards her.

Raymond's heart sank when he saw his beloved wife's wretched state. Her eyes trembled with rage above puffy sacks of darkened skin, a telltale sign of what must have been several sleepless nights. Her cheeks were drawn and her clothes wrinkled and stained. She gripped Gershom so tightly that Raymond worried she would smother the boy to death.

How dare you speak, Jael shouted, of agreeing to put your heads beneath the waters of defilement and of betraying the Holy One, Blessed be He? Don't you see He is testing us in this terrible hour, testing our faith, as Job was tested, as Abraham was tested? His wrath will be terrible if we fail this test, but if we do what should be done, His kindness and love for Israel will be overflowing.

When the Holy One tested Abraham, and told him to sacrifice his son, the one whom he loved, Isaac, Abraham did not hesitate, but led Isaac up the mountain and tied him to the altar. Isaac, too, willingly let himself be bound in obedience to the Holy One's will. Before Abraham could bring the knife down upon his son's neck, the flames on the altar underneath burned Isaac to a crisp.

The Holy One wept at this sacrifice and brought Isaac's charred remains to the Garden of Eden, where he spent three years healing until it was time for him to return home to marry Rebecca. When Satan lodges his accusations against Israel and tallies our many sins, and goads the wrath of the angels so that they demand the destruction of Israel for betraying the Holy One's Torah, it is Isaac who appears before the Throne of Glory and reminds Him of that great sacrifice. Because of the merit of Isaac's deed, the Holy One's wrath is appeased.

We too are being tested. Like Abraham, we face a choice: to obey the Holy One, Blessed be He, or to betray Him because we think, in our sinful hearts, we know better. I will not let these wicked men take my son and raise him in their lies and in their filth.

Jael reached out to the table near her—Bishop Adalbert's banqueting table—and grabbed a hunting knife. Blessed are You, Lord my God, King of the Universe, I offer You now this sacrifice as a witness for Israel against our many sins, as our Father Abraham did before me.

With these words, she plunged the knife into Gershom's breast and dropped him to the floor. He looked up at his mother in disbelief and shook violently as the life ebbed out of his small body. Jael bent down to embrace his bleeding, twitching chest as she wailed and moaned. Once Gershom had died, Jael stood up again with the bloody knife in her hand.

I wish now to sacrifice myself too, rather than be taken and defiled by the wicked men coming for us. Please, good Jews, someone take this knife and slit my throat so that I also may die as a righteous sacrifice.

After a pause in which no one stirred, a woman standing next to Jael took the hunting knife and cut her throat. Raymond watched, in helpless horror, as Jael's life bled out from her severed artery and her lifeless body fell on top of Gershom's corpse.

Now began an orgy of sacrifice. Knives glinted and flashed before Raymond's eyes as Jews cut one another down. A little girl ran to hide behind a desk in a corner, but her mother dragged her out, wailing and begging to be spared, and cut her down with a blood-stained dagger. Through the moans and screams of physical pain the Jews of Worms intoned the blessings from the ancient Temple in holy Jerusalem when animals were slaughtered upon the altar and their flesh offered up as sacrifices to the Holy One, Blessed be He.

When the Crusader knights reached Adalbert's hall, they recoiled in horror before the piles of dead bodies. They dropped their weapons, crossed themselves, and slowly staggered away.

The pool of water went black again, and then resumed its normal color. The mysterious force suddenly released its grip upon Raymond's body, causing him to fall to the ground. He stood up again with difficulty and quickly mounted the steps out of that subterranean chamber, eager to be far away from his demon wife. Raymond left the castle that day, and swore never to return through its gates.

He never saw the Lady Melusine again after that fateful Saturday morning. Through legend and gossip he later heard that she had walked into the castle's hall on the following Sunday morning, stood next to an open window, turned into a hawk and had flown away. Still, the servants insisted her spirit haunted the castle grounds, and in the wind they claimed to hear her lamentations.

IX. Ba'al Teshuvah

THE HOLY JEWISH communities of Ashkenaz (Germany) dreaded the visits of the wild beggar calling himself Solomon bar Shimson. In the persecutions of the year 1096 in the Christian calendar, the time of the First Crusade, many Jews in these communities had perished. Most of the survivors had preferred baptism to death, accepting conversion at sword-point as the ransom of their flesh. Once the troubles had subsided, the converts abandoned Christianity, rebuilt their homes and communities, sired a new generation of Jewish children, and placing one foot after the other, carried on.

Many of these former converts wished to forget those terrible days and their shameful weakness. But Solomon bar Shimson would not let them. This was not his actual name—he had abandoned his former name in shame at his own baptism in the year 1096. This man proclaimed himself a *ba'al teshuvah*, a master of repentance and return, reborn as Jewish wisdom (Solomon) sprung from Jewish strength (Shimson/Samson). As he never tired of telling any Jew he could corner, he had been a loathsome coward who had failed the Holy One's test of faith, befouling himself in the waters of defilement at the baptismal font instead of letting his throat be cut for *kiddush hashem*, the sanctification of the Holy Name. His wife, he would say mournfully, had been a righteous woman, a saint, who had killed herself and her child rather than submit to baptism. But he had failed in his faith.

Solomon bar Shimson was a terrifying figure. His hair and beard fell in tangled, dust-encrusted clumps and knots below his shoulders. His clothes were tattered and stained, and his feet covered with open, oozing sores from years of walking without shoes. Hunger—brought on by both voluntary fasts and extreme poverty—had hollowed his cheeks and made his eye sockets cavernous. He only slept upon grassy meadows and synagogue benches, leaving his joints stiff and hobbled.

Yet most remarkably he carried with him an ornate leather bag, far more elegant and expensive than any satchel possessed by any other Jew. Solomon bar Shimson said it was the last remaining spoil of his sinful past, but one that, out of necessity, he had to keep. For in this satchel, Solomon bar Shimson kept his most precious possession, his life's true work: a Hebrew manuscript setting forth every account he had gathered of the Jews' trials at the hands of the wicked Crusaders and the heroic stories of their holy martyrs who had refused baptism.

He would add to this manuscript each time he learned something new. And he was always learning something new, because in every town that he visited he demanded of every Jew whom he met to tell him what had happened in the year 1096 of the Christian calendar, what acts of persecution and deeds of valor must be recorded and remembered.

Nor was Solomon bar Shimson content with being himself the only repository of memory. In each town he visited, he would demand that the community's wealthy elite pay for a scribe to copy his manuscript in full, so that in that community the Jews would also remember. In some towns there was resistance to his request—after all, copying was expensive, and why was it needed? Everyone recalled the events of those awful days and would tell their children, who would, in turn, tell their own children, and so on and so forth from generation to generation.

Solomon bar Shimson's rattling bony frame would rise at these words, and he would hoarsely shout in his broken, rasping voice: Sinners! Wretches! You, who failed the test of faith, who in your cowardly shame ran away or took baptism rather than martyr yourselves for the sanctity and oneness of the Name of the Holy One, Blessed be He, you are not willing to part with any of your riches to record the deeds of the righteous? Your disgusting riches and carnal pleasures are only vouchsafed to you by the merit of those holy martyrs, may their memory be for a blessing, whose sacrifices and prayers have deflected the wrath of Heaven from your many and unending sins. Your worship of your riches is vile idolatry and lays bare the filthiness of the souls of men who would defile themselves with baptism rather than let their fat bellies suffer in the slightest. When you stand before the Heavenly Tribunal in the World to Come, your condemnation will be swift and your torments just.

Shamed by the mad beggar's angry words, the community elders would quietly agree to pay to copy the manuscript. Once the manuscript was copied and Solomon bar Shimson had mined that town's memory of the deeds of its holy martyrs and righteous saints, he would proceed to the next town. Sometimes he was offered alms, but he always returned any sum beyond what was necessary to purchase a ration of black bread, onions, and water.

Over the years, Solomon bar Shimson's efforts bore fruit. Not only was his own manuscript widely circulated, copied, and recited, but there were special memorial services held and candles lit to honor the martyrs. Poets took up their pens and crafted beautiful dirges for the fallen flowers of Israel, and these verses were sung in synagogues across Ashkenaz.

Yet Solomon bar Shimson did not live to see his labors come to their full realization. One day he lay down next to a road in a land that had been without a ruler for many years. Its lord and lady had both mysteriously vanished, and the bishop had maintained order as regent. But now the sons of the former lord, bold and glorious knights, had returned from many years of campaigns as Crusaders in the Holy Land to reclaim their patrimony. It was in this land, ruled by Crusader knights with blond locks and broad shoulders, that Solomon bar Shimson collapsed into slumber by the side of the road.

He woke with a terrible fright: A hawk was perched on top of his chest. The hawk's talons cut through his flimsy rags and tore into his skin. The hawk's eyes bore into him as if it were trying to figure out who this man was. Solomon bar Shimson attempted to break free, but to no avail—the bird possessed extraordinary strength and had him pinned.

After several minutes of this stalemate, the hawk let out a piercing scream full of anguish and rage. Solomon bar Shimson was rapidly encircled by armed men in hauberks. At the approach of these knights, the hawk released its grip and flew overhead, although the bird kept her eyes fixed firmly on him on the ground below.

He stood up tentatively, still bleeding from the wounds inflicted by the hawk's sharp talons. One of the knights bound him with rope and put him on back of a horse. With the hawk following them in the sky, the knights and their prisoner rode to a castle.

The knights brought him before their lords, Guyon and Renaud, recently returned from the Holy Land. The two young lords stopped discussing whatever they had been discussing as soon they laid eyes upon Solomon bar Shimson. Meanwhile, the hawk was circling around the outside of a high window facing into the room, tapping the panes now and then with her beak and claws.

Guyon and Renaud ordered their men to leave them alone with the prisoner. Once sure of their privacy, the brothers walked up to Solomon bar Shimson, examining him closely, almost sniffing him as if they were hunting dogs. Solomon closed his eyes and calmly mumbled prayers in Hebrew.

It is you, isn't it Father? Guyon asked.

I am not your father, my lord, Solomon said, I am a Jewish beggar, and not a Christian or a knight or a nobleman.

Guyon continued: Don't you recognize us? We are your sons. You are Count Raymond, lord of these lands. You were gone when we returned from our holy crusade in the lands of the Moslems. The bishop said you had departed without warning one day and had not been sighted since then. On our first night back here in our home, we both had the same dream: Our mother came to us and said she had been compelled to go away, but you were still wandering these lands, in disguise, pretending to be someone you are not. The hawk, she said, would reveal you to us. Follow the hawk. So we did, and so now we have you back. You can remove your absurd disguise—whatever danger made you flee is long gone—and assume your rightful place as lord of this castle and its estates. But tell us, who threatened you? Who is our enemy against whom we must strike back for reducing you to this state?

Solomon looked at Guyon, whose eyes were vibrating with excitement and hope. He sighed, sadly.

You have confused what is real and what is fake. I am really a Jew. I am really a beggar. I had one son, Gershom of blessed memory, who, because of our many sins, was martyred by the wicked for the sanctification of the Name of the Holy One, Blessed be He. But your eyes and your hawk have not wholly deceived you. I once pranced around this hall in masks and costumes, playing the part of a Christian nobleman. Yet it was a lie, born of black magic from a hideous demon. The Holy One sent His Prophet Elijah to bring me warning of the danger into which I had fallen. And then I saw your mother in her true form, with a serpent's tale for the bottom half of her body—a demon, no other explanation. No enemy drove me from this castle. Once the mist cleared from my eyes, I could no longer pretend that I was the man your demon mother had dressed me up to be. I left so that I could live as myself again, without falsity, and bear witness to the memory and suffering of the martyrs who sacrificed themselves for the Oneness of His Name in the year 1096.

Guyon and Renaud stepped back from their father. The three men were silent for several minutes. Solomon remained serene, even though his sons appeared to him to be deeply disturbed. Emotions flickered and faded on their faces: anger, sadness, fear, confusion, even love. But to Solomon these two men were the litter of a demon who had grown to be wicked knights, slaughtering the righteous in the name of their church's crusade. He saw no resemblance between him and them, either in soul or in body, and he was sure the demon woman had hatched them from her snake eggs without the use of his seed. They were not his children. They were more tricks, more phantoms, conjured by the demon lady's dark sorcery.

Guyon finally broke the silence: Why do you say such terrible and strange things? You are our father. How can you not love and care for your children? How can you slander the good name of our mother, who was so devoted and loyal to you? We are offering the opportunity to restore you to your rightful position. Stop this absurd farce. Be yourself again.

But I am myself. I am what I am, I will be what I will be, and that is a sad Jew doing penance for his many sins.

Once more, Solomon's voice was smug and remote. He betrayed no affection or concern for his sons.

Renaud drew his sword, approached his father, and pressed the sharp blade against his neck.

Enough of this madness, Renaud shouted. Take back your lies and slanders, or for the sake of my beloved mother's honor and good name I will run you through.

Solomon looked into Renaud's face quivering with rage. He saw a choice before him: Accept death as a Jew or life as a Christian nobleman. He saw again in his mind the vision of

Jael sacrificing their Gershom for *kiddush hashem*, the sanctification of the Holy Name.

Solomon's lips twisted into a spiteful grimace, and he
spoke with a hard, cruel edge to his voice: You are idol-
worshipping vermin, your Mary was an adulterer who con-
ceived your false Savior in sinful lust during her period of
impurity, and your mother was a filthy demon. I will not bow
to your idols, but like my wife and son of blessed memory, like
our father Isaac, I offer myself as a sacrifice in expiation for
our many sins and in witness to the Holy Name.

Renaud's grip slackened on his sword, but not before
Solomon purposefully drove his emaciated, leathery neck deep
into the sharp blade. Renaud dropped his sword and withdrew,
trembling in horror.

Solomon fell to the ground and smiled joyously at the
high ceiling stones, happy as his life ebbed away in the
knowledge that he had now, like Abraham and Isaac, passed
the great test of faith set by the Holy One, Blessed be He, and
earned himself a Golden Throne in Paradise.

Guyon and Renaud kneeled down over their father's
corpse. They embraced each other and wept profusely over the
sad end of their noble Christian father, who had been cursed
by the Devil with the affliction of madness. The brothers
arranged for a proper Christian burial for their father and for
masses sung in his honor for many years. Count Raymond's
grave and memory were honored by his sons, and by their sons
in turn, and the many sons thereafter of that noble house. He
eventually slipped into legend, and fabulous tales were told of
the noble, pious knight Raymond and the beautiful fairy
Melusine with her enchantments.

The Jews did not notice the disappearance of the hectoring, wandering beggar. But his manuscript, his chronicle of the terrible days of the year 1096 in the holy communities in the Rhineland and the heroic deeds of the martyrs, was read and copied and re-read and re-copied many times. It was later unearthed, edited, published, and dissected by scholars in the finest universities who, baffled by the lack of biographical evidence for Solomon bar Shimson, theorized the author's name was a fictitious personage, a literary ruse used by some scribe who stitched together various lost earlier source texts.

And so the real man faded into obscurity. But the lovely artifices have remained to be admired from generation to generation.

Other Books by Barak Bassman

Elegy of the Minotaur

Repentance: A Tale of Demons in Old Jewish Poland

King Solomon and Ashmedai: A Wisdom Tale

The Twilight of the Magical Siren: A Tale of Late Antiquity

The Leper Princess and The Court Jew

The Last Confession of Joseph della Reina